Original Korean text by Ji-yeong Lee
Illustrations by Gabriel Pacheco
Korean edition © Yeowon Media Co., Ltd.

This English edition published by big & SMALL in 2016
by arrangement with Yeowon Media Co., Ltd.
English text edited by Joy Cowley
English edition © big & SMALL 2016

Distributed in the United States and Canada by
Lerner Publishing Group, Inc.
241 First Avenue North
Minneapolis, MN 55401 U.S.A.
www.lernerbooks.com

All photo images used are in the public domain, except:
Page 39: "A production of Swan Lake by the Royal Swedish Opera (2008)"
© Alexander Kenney Kungliga Operan (CC BY 3.0)

ISBN: 978-1-925247-37-4

Printed in Korea

Tchaikovsky's

Swan Lake

Retold by Ji-yeong Lee
Illustrated by Gabriel Pacheco
Edited by Joy Cowley

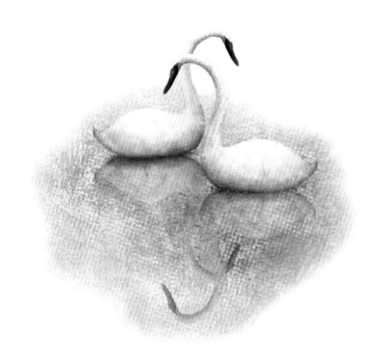

big & SMALL

Long ago, when magic was very powerful,
it could turn humans to animals and animals to humans.
It meant the evil sorcerer Count von Rothbart
could cast a spell over Princess Odette.
When the sun rose, she changed into a swan.
When the sun set, she became human again.
A vow of true love was the only way
to break the spell that held her.
Who would rescue Princess Odette?

Princess Odette

She is under a spell that turns her
into a swan during the day.

Prince Siegfried

He falls in love with Odette.

Count von Rothbart

He is a sorcerer who cast the spell on Odette, and wants the prince to marry his daughter, not Odette.

Odile

Count von Rothbart's cold and arrogant daughter.

5

There was a party at the palace
to celebrate Prince Siegfried's twenty-first birthday.
In the middle of it, the queen appeared.
She said to the prince, "My son, you are the future king.
It is time for you to choose a wife who will be queen.
Tomorrow night, I am hosting a grand ball
and I've invited several princesses.
You must choose one to be your bride."

The prince's heart was heavy.
How could he marry someone he didn't love?
He went out into the garden with his friends
and saw a flock of swans flying across the sky.
His friends suggested that he go swan hunting
to try out his new bow, which was a birthday gift.
The prince and his friends got on their horses
and followed the swans into the forest.

Leaving his friends,
the prince walked along the shore of the lake.
The swans flew overhead and came down,
one by one, onto the lake's surface.
The prince took aim with his bow and arrow.
But suddenly the swans were surrounded by light
and they began to change into beautiful women
who walked gracefully out of the water.
The prince was so surprised, he dropped his bow.

One woman shone brighter than the others.
The prince moved closer to her and said,
"I am Prince Siegfried. Who are you?"

The woman replied in a soft voice,
"I am Princess Odette. My ladies and I
are under a sorcerer's evil spell.
When the sun comes up, we turn into swans.
At night, we turn back into humans."

The prince asked how the spell could be broken.

Odette replied that it could only be broken
by a vow of true love.

The prince took Odette's hand. "I promise you,
I will kill the sorcerer who made this spell."

Odette explained that if the sorcerer was killed,
the spell could never be broken.

The prince said, "I will love you and protect you.
Come to the ball at the palace tomorrow night
and I will choose you as my bride."

The prince and Odette spent a happy time together,
but all too soon it was morning. The sun rose,
and Odette and the other women turned into swans.
The prince watched as they flew into the sky.

Also watching was an owl in a tree.
The owl was the sorcerer in disguise.

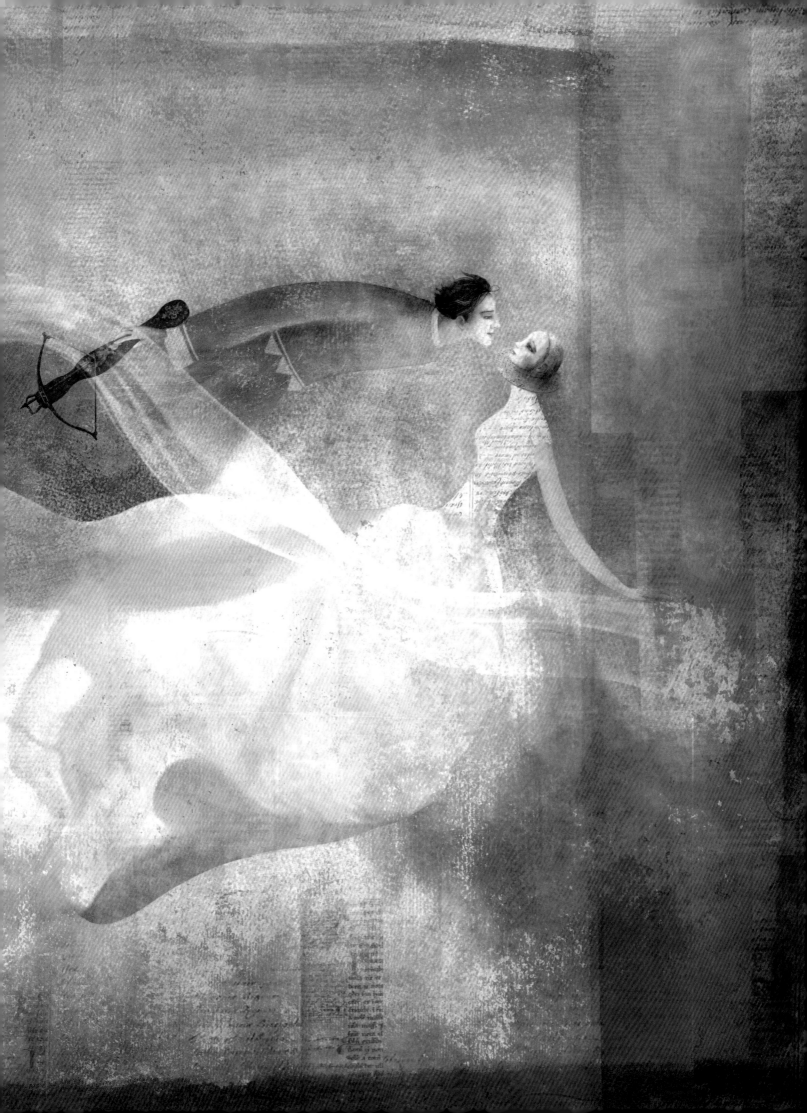

It was time for the grand ball,
and princesses arrived from other countries.
At the queen's orders,
the prince danced with each princess,
but his heart was with Princess Odette.

He longed for her to come to the ball
so he could introduce her to the queen
as the one he has chosen to be his bride.

The trumpets sounded, and it was announced,
"Count von Rothbart and his daughter!"
A man and a beautiful woman wearing black came in.
The prince was very surprised to see them.
The woman looked exactly like Odette,
except for the color of her dress.
The prince cried, "Odette, my love!"

However, the count was the sorcerer,
and the woman was not Odette.
The count had made magic on his daughter
so that Odile looked like Odette.

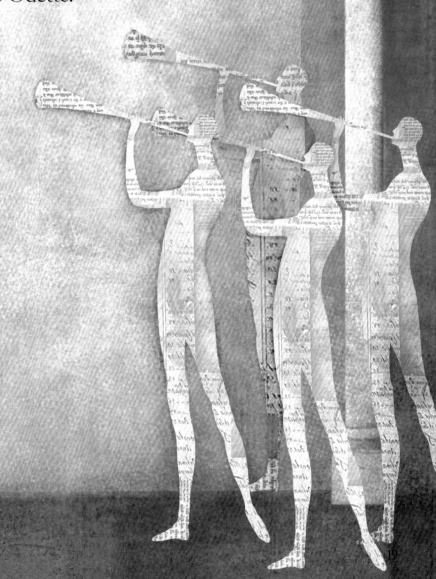

Prince Siegfried asked Odile for a dance,
believing she was Odette.
He whispered, "I love you, Odette.
I want to marry you."

Odile smiled and did not say a single word.
She simply danced to the beautiful music.

The queen, watching the couple dance,
was delighted at her son's interest.

Holding Odile's hand, the prince went to the queen.
"Mother, this is Princess Odette. I want to marry her."
At that moment, someone knocked on the window.

The real Odette, dressed in white,
was standing outside, crying.
The prince looked at the two women
and realized he had been tricked.
His body trembled with distress.

The count and Odile sneered in triumph
as they walked away from the ballroom.

Odette ran back to the lake blindly
where she told her ladies-in-waiting
what had happened at the palace.
"Everything is over! All hope is gone!"
she cried as the ladies stopped Odette
from throwing herself into the lake.

After a while, Odette calmed down
and thought about the prince.

When the prince followed Odette to the lake,
the evil count tried to stop him with magic.
The prince was scratched by tree branches,
and he fell over a stone. Rain beat down on him.
There was thunder and lightning.
But nothing could stop Prince Siegfried.

Shedding tears, the prince said to Odette,
"Please forgive me. I thought she was you."

Odette ran to the prince and hugged him.
"It is not your fault, dear Siegfried.
You were tricked by the sorcerer."

The prince thought all would be well,
but Odette shook her head. "No!
Nothing remains for me now
but to stay a swan forever."

The prince said, "I will be with you forever,
for my love for you is stronger than anything."

The count appeared out of the deep, dark forest.
He sneered at the prince and reminded him
that he had already broken his promise to Princess Odette.
Then the count took a long breath and blew a gale.
The prince and Odette could not open their eyes.
The ladies-in-waiting were scattered by the wind,
and the waves on the lake rose up to swallow Odette.

The prince dived into the lake to rescue her.

Suddenly, the count was screaming with pain.
Then he disappeared like smoke in the air.
He had been defeated by the power of true love.

The prince had swum through the water
and saved his beloved Odette.
At that moment the spell was broken,
and the sorcerer destroyed.

Prince Siegfried and Princess Odette
returned to the palace to be married,
and looked forward to a happy future.

𝄞: Let's Learn About **Swan Lake**

🎹 Pyotr Ilyich Tchaikovsky

Born: 7 May 1840

Died: 6 November 1893

Place of birth: Votkinsk, Russia

Biography: Tchaikovsky was a famous Russian composer whose works included symphonies, concertos, operas, and ballets. His musical talent was obvious from his first piano lessons at the age of five. However, it was not until he was twenty-two that he enrolled in the Saint Petersburg Conservatory to study music. After graduating from the conservatory, he started his career as a professional composer. Tchaikovsky composed works in which Russian melodies were mixed with European music techniques.

Tchaikovsky's ballet music is especially praised for being well-organized and artistic. Tchaikovsky's three major ballet works, *Swan Lake, The Sleeping Beauty*, and *The Nutcracker*, are still performed all over the world. Tchaikovsky died in 1893, shortly after finishing his *Symphony No. 6 in B Minor*, which was played at his funeral.

A part of the score of Tchaikovsky's *Swan Lake*.

The Story of **Swan Lake**

Swan Lake performed by the Bolshoi Ballet in 1901.

Swan Lake is a ballet Tchaikovsky composed at the request of the Bolshoi Theater in 1875. Based on a European fairy tale, *Swan Lake* tells the story of Odette, a princess turned into a swan by the curse of an evil sorcerer. The premiere of *Swan Lake* in 1877 was not well-received, and the work was soon forgotten. But in 1895, when *Swan Lake* was performed at the Mariinsky Theater in Saint Petersburg, it became a big hit.

It remains one of the most beloved ballet works worldwide today. *Swan Lake* is performed differently by creating new endings or presenting characters in new ways. In 1995, an English choreographer called Matthew Bourne put on *Swan Lake* using only male dancers. If you ever go to see *Swan Lake*, look closely at the dance of Odile disguised as Odette, where she pirouettes thirty-two times without stopping.

Anna Sobeshchanskaya as Odette at the premiere in 1877.

A production of *Swan Lake* by the Royal Swedish Ballet (2008).

♫ Let's Find Out About the Music

Swan Lake originally contained thirty-six pieces of music and the most popular six pieces have been made into a ballet suite. Let's find out about the music and its imagery of beautiful swans upon a lake.

Waltz

"Waltz" is the dance music played at the party celebrating the prince's birthday. Princesses come from many countries to try to gain the prince's attention and become his bride. The splendid atmosphere of the party and the movement of beautiful dresses are shown in this piece.

Scene

The main melody of "Scene" describes the mood of *Swan Lake*, and it reappears many times throughout the work. It represents the scene at the foggy lake where the enchanted swans swim.

Dance of the Little Swans

This piece is played when the swans are dancing delightfully at the news that the prince has invited Princess Odette to the party. It describes the swans' excitement cheerfully and rhythmically, reflecting the scene of swans swimming lightly on the water.

The Dances of Swans

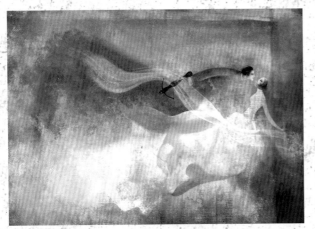

"The Dances of Swans" is a piece where the violin plays the main melody as the harp creates a mysterious atmosphere based on the harmony of the woodwind. The woodwind then play a cheerful melody, followed by the duet of the cello and the violin.

Hungarian Dance

At his birthday party, although the prince is dancing with other princesses, he thinks only about Princess Odette. This piece captures the prince's wandering mind as he dances with the other princesses.

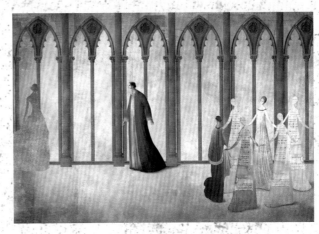

Scene Finale

The orchestra plays the main melody again powerfully, telling of the happy ending of the prince who has kept his vow and the princess whose spell is broken.

Let's Discover the Secrets of Ballet

Ballet is a type of performance dance expressing a story with body movements to the music. The special clothing and shoes worn by the dancers and the different body gestures are very interesting and help bring the ballet to life. Let's find out more about them.

Marie Taglioni wearing a tutu for the first time in *La Sylphide*.

Tutu

A female dancer in a ballet performance is called ballerina, and she wears a tutu. This tradition began in 1832 when the ballerina Marie Taglioni danced in a bell-shaped skirt made of layers of stiffened fabric. This dress gave the illusion of fullness, but it was very light for the dancer to wear.

It became known as the tutu and it was soon the standard costume for ballerinas. As the movements of ballet grew more difficult, the tutu became shorter to show the dancers' fancy footwork. It also changed shape to come out vertically at the waist, instead of down over the legs.

Pointe shoes

How can ballerinas stand on tiptoes without falling over? They wear special shoes called "pointe shoes" because dancing done on tiptoes is called "pointe work." The tips of the shoes are flat and hard, so they make it easier for ballerinas to stand on tiptoes. Although ballerinas look graceful to the audience when they stand in this position, it makes the feet of ballerinas very sore.

Pointe shoes

Body Gestures in Ballet

Ballet expresses a story using body movements and gestures to the music. These are the meanings of some of the gestures.

Pray
Holding two hands together as if praying.

Marriage
Pointing to the ring finger of the left hand with the right hand.

Calling
Raising one hand and as if calling someone.

Vow
With the left hand on the heart, raising the right arm with the index finger and the middle finger pointing to the sky.

Refusal
Pushing outward with crossed hands, while turning in the opposite direction.

Love
Placing hands gently together on the chest.

Listening
Cupping the ear gently with the palm.